Contents

Prologue 1

1 The Table 7

2 The Kitchen 17

3 Chairs 25

4 The Kitchen Again 39

5 Preparations 51

6 The All Knight Party! 58

7 The Stable Yard 74

THE CAST

KING ARTIE

QUEEN GWINNY

THE KNIGHTS

SIR PRANCELOT . . . . the keen one

SIR PERCY . . . . the fussy one

SIR GARY . . . . the gloomy one

SIR TRALAHAD . . . . the musical one

SIR BORE DE GANNET . . . ze French one

SIR ANGELA . . . . she's a girl in disguise

THE STAFF

OLD TOBY . . . . the gardener

SHAWN . . . . the odd job boy

MRS SPUNGE . . . . the cook

AGGIE . . . . the serving wench

The Knights of the Drop-Leaf Table

Kaye Umansky

With illustrations by
Ben Whitehouse

To Mo and Ella

First published in 2017 in Great Britain by
Barrington Stoke Ltd
18 Walker Street, Edinburgh, EH3 7LP

www.barringtonstoke.co.uk

Text © 2017 Kaye Umansky
Illustrations © 2017 Ben Whitehouse

A CIP catalogue record for this book is available
from the British Library upon request

ISBN: 978-1-78112-690-5

Printed in China by Leo

THE CASTLE ANIMALS

ETHEL . . . . the cat

BOB . . . . the dog

THE HORSES

STOP-A-LOT . . . . who stops a lot

LIGHTNING . . . . the slow one

BREAKWIND . . . . don't stand behind him

ELTON . . . . she's a mare

LOUD WINNIE . . . . the noisy one

GNASHER . . . . he bites

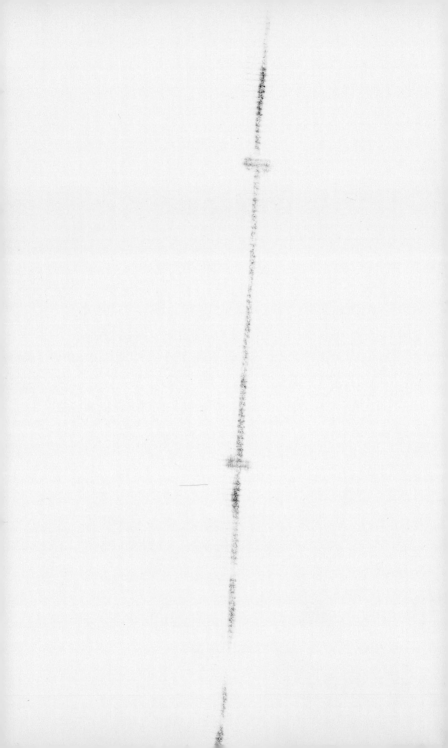

Prologue

It was breakfast time at Castle Llamalot, but the King wasn't eating. Most days, he went for the full Olde Englishe. Griffin kidneys, dumplings of boar tail, swan fritters, poached partridge in a pear tree sauce – he could put all that away with no trouble. But not this morning.

"What's the matter, dear?" the Queen asked, as she spread honey on her toast. "No appetite?"

"No," the King said, with a sigh. "Not really. The knights are getting to me."

"Don't eat cheese before bed time," the Queen said. "I keep telling you, Artie."

"No, not the *nights*. The Knights."

"Oh, right," the Queen said. "Yes, well, I must admit, they are rather annoying. Cluttering up the corridors. Leaving their pikes and swords sticking out for people to trip over. And so *noisy*."

"Exactly," said the King. "And they never leave me *alone*, Gwinny! I can't walk anywhere without them clanking after me, demanding things. They want me to send them off on quests or organise another jousting tournament or test them on the Code of Chivalry. I can't even visit the privy without one of them knocking on the door asking if I'll be long because he's written another poem. Listen to this rubbish."

The King pulled a scroll from his sleeve and unrolled it.

Roses are red, snowdrops are white,

You are the King and I am a knight.

With a hey-nonny-no and a skip-too-maloo,

Here ends verse one, but I plan twenty-two.

"That's Sir Tralahad's latest." The King rolled the scroll up again. "He's going to set it to music and sing it at the next banquet."

"What – all twenty-two verses?" the Queen said.

"I'm afraid so."

"In that reedy voice of his? Oh, no, Artie! Tell him we don't want music this time. Be nice, but be firm."

"I tried to, but he looked so *hurt*." The King buried his head in his hands in despair. "All of them look hurt when I turn them down, no matter how nice I am. It's driving me up the

3

wall, Gwinny. I don't think I can put up with much more."

"Ban them from the corridors, then, darling," the Queen said. "You're the King."

"But that's *mean*. Kings shouldn't be mean."

"They're overcrowding the corridors," the Queen pointed out. "It's not mean to ban them. It's practical."

"But where will they go?"

"I don't know. Give them a room somewhere."

"A room?" The King looked up. "Do we have a spare room?"

"I'm sure we can find one." The Queen chewed her toast, deep in thought. "A nice, private little room they can relax in. A comfy sofa. Candles in bottles. Maybe a small area for dancing. A sort of Knight Club."

"If they relaxed on a comfy sofa they'd never get up again," said the King. "Not in all that armour. And I can't see them dancing either."

"All right, forget the sofa. Give them hard chairs. And a big manly table to sit at."

"They'll only squabble about who'll sit at the head of it," the King groaned. "You know how competitive they are with their manliness."

"Make it a round one. Then they're all equal. It's not catapult science, Artie."

"Hmmm." The King looked thoughtful. "You know, Gwinny, you just might be onto something. Do we have a round table in the castle?"

Chapter 1
The Table

"Wow!" said Sir Prancelot, as he pushed back his visor and looked around. "Zounds, odds-boddikins and double *wowzeree*! This is it. Our very own room! What do we think, guys?"

Six knights stood in a cluster of metal, surveying the empty room. Stone walls. Stone floor. A small, grubby window. Cobwebs. Funny smell.

Hmm.

"Tra la LAAA!" Sir Tralahad burst out, making everyone jump. "One, two, one, two, TESTING! As I feared. Poor acoustics. Too much echo."

"Filthy," said Sir Percy. He clanked to the window and ran a fussy finger along the sill. "I can't imagine what it was used for."

"Ze store room for ze old, rotten vegetables, by ze steenky smell," said Sir Bore de Gannet, who was French. "You Engleesh. Always ze bad food."

"Some curtains would be nice," said Sir Angela, who was a girl in disguise.

Nobody liked to say anything. One of the rules in the Code of Chivalry was that you had to be polite to girls. Besides, Angela had gone to a lot of trouble. She had cut her hair short and she insisted that they pronounce her name with a hard G, like in Grapefruit. Sir AnGela.

Sometimes, when she remembered, she drew a small moustache on her top lip.

"It's a dump," said Sir Gary, who could always be relied upon to make the worst of things.

"Hey! Guys!" Sir Prancelot cried. "Come on! Where's your gratitude? We've got a room, yah? This is awesome! We can put in a dartboard! A bar! Make it our own."

"I don't know about bars and dartboards," Sir Percy said with a frown. "The room is intended for serious business meetings. A place to discuss important knightly affairs. We need to get some office furniture in." He whipped out a small notebook with a pencil attached from behind his breastplate. "A notice board and a blackboard. An amusing sign that says *You Don't Have To Be Mad To Work Here But It Helps*. An umbrella stand for the swords. I'll make a list."

"Didn't Her Majesty say something about a round table?" Sir Tralahad asked.

"She did," said Sir Percy. "And if I'm not mistaken, here it comes now!"

Noises were indeed coming from the corridor. The sound of something large scraping against the wall. And a bad-tempered voice they knew well – Old Toby, the gardener.

"Up a bit, Shawn. To your right. *Right*, I said, dimbo," Old Toby was grumbling. "No, don't drop it, don't drop it, you daft little – hang on, I'm losing it – arrgh! Was that yer fingers? Ah, you'll live. Right, steady 'er up. Lean 'er against the wall. I'll get the door."

The door crashed open to reveal Old Toby and Shawn, the odd job boy. Both of them looked hot, bothered and unhappy. Old Toby was rubbing his back. Shawn was sucking his squashed fingers.

"Aha!" Sir Prancelot cried. "Good day to you, old grey beard. Our thanks for this kind service! How goes it, young shaver?" He reached out his hand in its metal gauntlet to ruffle Shawn's carroty hair. Shawn smacked it away. Not in the mood.

"Whatever," Old Toby growled. "Mind out, we're comin' in."

The knights clanked out of the way.

Old Toby and Shawn went back out to the corridor, then reappeared carrying between them a large and awkward piece of furniture. Everyone craned forward as it advanced into the room.

"There you go," Old Toby said, standing back. "One table. And a blasted pig of a thing it were to get 'ere."

The knights stared. It was a table all right. It was made of wood. The wood had been polished. And it was big. A big, wooden, polished table. But –

"I don't want to criticise, yah?" said Sir Prancelot. "But we were kind of sort of led to believe it would be round? You know. Like, circular?"

"So?" said Old Toby.

"Well, it's not a round table, is it? It's half a circle."

"That's because it's a drop-leaf," Old Toby said smugly. He might not be a knight, but he knew about tables. "See, one half stays up an' the half with the hinges drops down. So you can get it through doors. It's got a moveable leg under what you pulls out to prop up the flap. Show 'em, Shawn."

In a sulk, Shawn showed them how the table worked.

"See?" Old Toby said. "Now it's round."

"I say," said Sir Prancelot. "That's jolly clever. Look at that, guys! That's brilliant!"

"It's rubbish," said Sir Gary.

"It'd look better with a table cloth," Sir Angela said. "And a vase of flowers."

"I don't *think* so, Angela," said Sir Percy. "I mean Sir AnGela. We're knights, not members of the Queen's sewing circle. But we will need some chairs."

"Chairs are comin'," Old Toby said. "Give us a chance."

"This is a moment we must celebrate," Sir Tralahad said. He picked up his lyre. "I feel a new song coming on ...

Gather round and hear my fable

All about a drop-leaf table,

Fal diddle dee and a ninny nonny no ..."

The Queen was right. Sir Tralahad's singing got on people's nerves in a very short space of time. His lyre playing wasn't too hot either.

"We'll get the chairs," Old Toby said, keen to get out as fast as he could. "Come on, Shawn."

"Time for ze lunch, non?" said Sir Bore de Gannet. "Anybody care to join me?"

"We should wait for the chairs," Sir Percy said. "Rude to push off when they're going to so much trouble."

"You Engleesh!" Sir Bore de Gannet grumbled. "No respect for ze proper meal times!"

But he made no move to leave. All of them wanted to try sitting around the new table. Even Sir Gary, for all he'd never admit it.

"*Gather round and hear my fable ...*" Sir Tralahad tried again.

"No, Tralahad," said Sir Percy. "Not now."

"Yeah," said Sir Gary. "Put a sock in it."

Chapter 2
The Kitchen

"'Ere!" said Mrs Spunge, the cook. "Where you goin' with my chairs?"

"They're needed upstairs," Old Toby said. "For the new knights' room. Their club, you know."

"So what are we supposed to sit on?" said Mrs Spunge.

"I'll bring in the bench from the garden," said Old Toby.

"I don't want to sit on a nasty old bench," Mrs Spunge spluttered. "I want my proper chairs."

Old Toby shook his head. "Just followin' orders, Mrs S. Don't blame me. Off you go, Shawn. I'll be up in a minute."

"You put that chair down, Shawn." Mrs Spunge marched to the doorway and folded her floury arms. "That chair's going nowhere."

"That's right, Mrs S, you tell 'em," said Aggie the kitchen wench. "Flippin' cheek. Taking our chairs."

"Look," said Old Toby. "I got me orders. If you got any complaints, go and see the Queen. She's organising it all."

"Organising what all?"

Old Toby sighed. "I told yer. The knights are gettin' a new room."

"What do they need a room for?" Mrs Spunge asked.

"Don't ask me. Meetin's and that."

"Oh." Mrs Spunge gave a sigh. She had a lot of respect for the Queen. "Well, all right, then. Seein' it's 'er Majesty. But you can bring that bench in right now. And scrape the nasty moss and bird droppin's off it an' all. This is my kitchen and I got rules about keepin' things clean."

She stamped back to the table and began to pluck a chicken.

"Will do," said Old Toby. It didn't do to upset the cook. "Oh, by the way, I got a note for you. From the Queen."

"Well, you could have said! Give it here, then."

Mrs Spunge held out a hand covered in feathers and Old Toby rummaged in his huge pockets. At last he hunted down a small, rolled-up parchment.

"Ooh," Aggie said. "A note from 'er Majesty 'erself. What's it say, Mrs S?"

"*Dear Mrs Spunge,*" Mrs Spunge read. "*You may have heard that the knights are to have a new meeting room. I wonder if you could supply them with mid-morning tea and perhaps a plate of your delicious home-made biscuits. Thank you so much. By the way, last night's roast cockatrice was wonderful. All good wishes, Your Queen.*"

"Aw," Aggie said. "Isn't that nice?"

"Don't say nothing about chairs." Mrs Spunge sniffed. "Get down, Bob, you're not havin' any more."

Bob was the castle dog. Unlike the King, he had a huge appetite on this day and every other. He'd scoffed his breakfast in two great gulps and was hoping for seconds. But it wasn't to be. Everyone was standing around shouting about chairs.

Oh well. Time for a walkabout. Dustbins first, just in case.

Bob trotted out of the kitchen and sniffed around the bins, which had their lids on tight as usual.

Then he trampled across the vegetable garden, dug up a couple of lettuces just for fun, lifted a leg against a tree and barked at a squirrel.

Then he moved on to the pond, lapped some water, snapped at a couple of frogs but missed, then sat back, had a little scratch and wondered what to do next.

Look for the cat, that was what. The cat was always good for a laugh.

Bob put his nose to the ground and set off in search of Ethel, the castle cat.

Chapter 3
Chairs

"Huzzah!" Sir Prancelot cried, and he brandished his sword. "Chairs! Here they come!"

The knights stood back as Old Toby and Shawn staggered in, each with three stacked chairs. They dumped them on the flagstones, then proceeded to place them around the table. Three went on the half that was always up, and three on the side with the hinged drop leaf.

"Chairs," Old Toby announced. "Come on, Shawn, let's go before they thinks of anythin' else."

The moment the door closed, all the knights made an un-knightly rush for the chairs on the fixed side. Sir Prancelot, Sir Percy and Sir Gary won. Sir Angela, Sir Tralahad and Sir Bore de Gannet were slower off the mark, and so they were left standing, eyeing the three remaining chairs with deep suspicion.

"Well!" said Sir Angela. "Talk about rude." She glared at Sir Prancelot. "That was my foot you trod on!"

"I 'ave a good mind to call you out, Sir! For pushing!" Sir Bore de Gannet declared to Sir Percy, with his hand on his sword hilt.

"I didn't push," Sir Percy lied.

"Yes, you did," said Sir Tralahad and Sir Angela.

"I did *not*." Sir Percy placed his notepad on the table with the pencil lined up next to it. "Sit down, Sirs. There's a chair for everybody. Three left."

"Yes," Sir Angela said in a cold voice. "On the worst side."

"What d'you mean, worst side?" Sir Percy said.

"The side with the drop leaf, of course."

"Right!" Sir Bore de Gannet agreed. His armour squealed as he stooped and peered underneath. "Zis under-leg made by Engleesh man. Ees no good. Eet bend, eet shake. Kick eet by accident, and whoosh! Ze flap, eet fall down."

"Don't kick it, then," Sir Percy advised.

"Honestly," said Sir Prancelot. "You guys. As if it makes a difference which side we're on."

"In that case, I'll sit where you are," said Sir Angela.

"Ah, come on, Angela," Sir Prancelot pleaded. "I mean, Sir AnGela." It was one thing to sit down in armour. Getting up again was something else. "I'm here now."

"And I've got my things set out," Sir Percy said.

"Don't expect me to move," said Sir Gary. He was cleaning his fingernails with the point of his sword.

"So much for the Code of Chivalry!" Sir Angela pulled out a chair and sat down with a cross clang.

Sir Tralahad and Sir Bore de Gannet did the same, with very bad grace. All three were careful to keep their hands, elbows, knees, pikes, swords, feet and lyre tucked well away

from the table. Nobody wanted to be the cause of a terrible accident.

"Well, here we all are, guys," Sir Prancelot said, beaming round. "Our first meeting in our fabulous new room. Sitting around our amazing new table. What shall we talk about?"

"Well, first, we should decide what needs to be done with the room," Sir Percy said. He picked up his pencil. "I've written down *blackboard*, *notice board*, *umbrella stand* and *amusing sign*. And get the place cleaned up, of course. A servant can do that."

"The Code of Chivalry needs to be framed and hung on the wall," Sir Angela said, with a glare at Sir Prancelot. "Some people need to be reminded of its rules."

"Hear, hear!" Sir Tralahad and Sir Bore de Gannet chorused.

The fact they had been forced to sit on the unpopular side of the table really hadn't gone down at all well. There was still a lot of resentment in the air.

"Good thinking, Angela," Sir Percy said. "I mean, Sir AnGela. *I* don't need to be reminded of the Code, of course. I know the rules by heart."

"What are zey, zen?" Sir Bore de Gannet demanded. "Go on, if you're so clever."

"Don't Murder Anyone," Sir Percy said. "That's number one."

"Yah," said Sir Prancelot. "Jolly good. Top rule, that."

"Don't Commit Treason," Sir Percy went on, ticking them off on his fingers. "Grant Mercy To Those Who Ask For It. Help Women If They Need It."

"Only the posh ones," Sir Gary said.

"Well, yes, that's obvious. And the final two are Don't Be Mean and Always Be Polite." Sir Percy sat back, pleased with himself.

"Hah! See? Be Polite!" said Sir Angela. "Always."

Sir Prancelot went a bit pink, but he still didn't offer her his chair.

"*Hey nonny nonny, and a table-o!*" Sir Tralahad warbled, and he picked up his lyre.

"Not now, Tralahad," said Sir Percy. "It's not the time for singing. We're trying to get down to some serious business."

"*You* are," said Sir Tralahad. "I'm a free-spirited poet-musician and I'm tired of talking about office furniture and rules. What we should be doing is planning this evening. We should have a merry celebration."

"By jove, he's right!" Sir Prancelot cried, and he banged a metal fist on the table. The drop-leaf half jumped up and down. "Are we not knights? Let's make a night of it! *Party! Party!* Come on, guys, join in. *Party! Party!*"

"Don't bang the table like that," Sir Angela snapped. "You're making it wobble."

"Sorry, sorry," Sir Prancelot said. "My apologies. In fact, sorry about earlier, yah? I forgot my manners as a knight. Sorry I trod on your foot, Angela. I mean Sir AnGela. Please take my chair."

"I don't want it now," said Sir Angela.

"A celebration is a good idea," said Sir Percy. He was a little bit annoyed, because he hadn't thought of it first. "I was about to suggest it myself. I'll make a note to order up some party food from the kitchen."

"Zat Spunge woman!" Sir Bore de Gannet burst out. "Zat *cook*! She rubbeesh. Your Engleesh cooks, zey know nuzzink. Nuzzink but ze stodge and ze soggy vegetables. Pah!"

"Are you talkin' about Mrs Spunge?" a pert new voice said from the door. It was Aggie the kitchen wench, with a tray.

"*Oui*," said Sir Bore de Gannet. "Yes."

"So you won't be wanting the tea and biscuits she's sent up, then?" Aggie said.

"Ah!" cried Sir Percy. "Light refreshments! Or should I say, *knight* refreshments, ha, ha! Hear what I did there? No, no, by all means leave them here, girl."

"Splendid!" Sir Prancelot agreed, and he clapped his hands together with a clang. "A tasty snack, what ho!"

"I bet the tea's cold," said Sir Gary.

"*Tea!*" Sir Bore de Gannet spat. "Away wiz your milky Engleesh tea like water from ze sink and your nasty Engleesh biskeets zat break ze teeth! Huh."

"Thanks, Aggie," Sir Angela said. "Tell Mrs Spunge we're very grateful."

Everyone watched with bated breath as Aggie set down the tray in the middle of the table. It was the first time that any weight had been placed on the drop-leaf side. This was a test. The drop-leaf tilted a bit, but it held.

"Very good." Sir Percy sniffed. "Now bring up a dustpan and brush. This place is filthy."

Aggie sniffed back at him and flounced out.

Sir Angela glared at Sir Percy and Sir Bore de Gannet. "I think you're both very rude."

"But ees true," said Sir Bore de Gannet. "I demonstrate." He stretched across the table and grabbed a biscuit. The drop-leaf flap wobbled.

"*Careful!*" Sir Angela and Sir Tralahad cried.

Sir Bore de Gannet bared his sharp little teeth and attempted to bite down on the biscuit. The surface was not even scratched. Mrs Spunge always added a secret ingredient (sawdust) to the mix, to make it go further.

"Uggh. You see?" He threw it over his shoulder. "Deesgusteeng. Where are ze warm croissants? Ze crusty baguettes? Ze delicious pastries? Us French can cook you Engleesh into ze corner."

"Is that right? Show us, then," Sir Angela challenged. "If you're so good, why don't *you* cook tonight's feast?"

"Good call!" Sir Prancelot cried. "A noble French banquet, yah, prepared by Sir Bore's noble French hands! I'm up for that!"

"I've never tried French food," Sir Percy said. He looked rather doubtful. "I've heard it's very rich."

"I've heard it's very horrible," said Sir Gary. He helped himself to a cup and took a sip of tea. "Yep. Stone cold, just as I thought."

"So," said Sir Angela. "What d'you say, Sir Bore? Up to the challenge?"

"Challenge?" Sir Bore de Gannet squealed. "Since when 'as a Frenchman turned down a challenge? Besides, for me, ees not a challenge. Ees – 'ow you say? – a doddle. I learn to cook at my mama's knee!"

He crashed to his feet, banging the table, which wobbled again. Tea slopped all over the tray.

"*Careful!*" everybody chorused.

Sir Bore clanked to the door, and paused.

"Gentlemen," he announced, "I will prepare a feast like you 'ave never eaten!"

The sound of his footsteps could be heard clanking away down the corridor.

"It'll be horrible," Sir Gary said. "Very horrible."

Chapter 4
The Kitchen Again

Mrs Spunge stared at Sir Bore de Gannet. "What d'you mean, you want to prepare a feast?" she said.

Sir Bore was wearing a striped apron over his suit of armour, and he had replaced his helmet with a tall chef's hat. He had thrown down his gauntlets and in each hand he held a bucket covered with cloth.

"You 'eard," Sir Bore de Gannet said. "I am about to prepare ze traditional French feast for zis evening. Eet will be served in ze new

meeting room, on ze new drop-leaf table. So get out of ze kitchen, woman, and give me space."

"I'll do no such thing," said Mrs Spunge. "What's in them buckets?"

"Ingredients," said Sir Bore de Gannet, and he plonked the buckets next to the sink. "Ze snails and ze frogs."

"Yuck," said Aggie, who had come in to collect the dustpan and brush. "Are you serious?"

"I'm not havin' them nasty slimy things in 'ere," said Mrs Spunge. "Get 'em out, this minute."

Ethel the castle cat had wandered in and was sitting next to her dish. Like Bob, she was hoping it would fill up again by some miracle. Like Bob, she was disappointed. Everyone was too busy shouting about buckets.

"I am a knight, madame." Sir Bore de Gannet sniffed. "I think you will find zat outranks ze cook. Go!"

"Oh, I'm going, all right," Mrs Spunge snapped, red with fury. She untied her apron and flung it on the bench. "I'm going to complain to the Queen! How's my hair lookin', Aggie?"

"Lovely," said Aggie. "All yellow and fluffy, like one of your nice sponges."

Mrs Spunge banged out.

"I'm off to clean your new meeting room," Aggie told Sir Bore de Gannet. "I'll leave you to it. Snails. Yuck."

Sir Bore de Gannet stared around the empty kitchen and rubbed his hands in satisfaction. He was looking forward to this.

His eye fell on Ethel, who was still crouched by her dish in hope.

"Cat," said Sir Bore de Gannet. "Scat!"

Ethel did. She knew when she wasn't wanted.

Ethel led a life of routine. She spent it doing four things – eating, sleeping, sun-bathing and avoiding Bob the dog. She had already eaten and didn't feel like sleeping. There was a maniac in the kitchen. Bob was sniffing around the garden. She decided to have a wander up to the castle ramparts and find a warm spot where she could flop down and watch the birds in peace. Bob wouldn't find her up there. He wasn't allowed upstairs.

*

Aggie walked down the corridor to the knights' new meeting room, with dustpan and brush in hand. The door crashed open and four knights came clanking out. Three of them looked rather excited. The fourth didn't. Sir Gary didn't do excitement.

Aggie stood back to allow them to clang by.

"I must say, I'm looking forward to this!" Sir Prancelot cried. "Our first ever All Knight Party. Feasting! Laughter!"

"And music," added Sir Tralahad.

"But I'm not at all sure about this French feast business," said Sir Percy. "I have a delicate stomach. I shall order back-up jelly and buns from Mrs Spunge. And a jug of her best lemonade to toast their majesties."

"Huzzah!" Sir Prancelot cried. "Such larks! Feasting, laughter *and* toasting!"

"And music," Sir Tralahad reminded him again. "I shall be performing my new table song."

"Bor-*ing*," Sir Gary said, with a yawn.

"Are you insulting me, Sir?" Sir Tralahad demanded.

"I might be," said Sir Gary. "Want to make something of it?"

"Ah, come on, guys, don't be like that!" Sir Prancelot soothed. "This is a fun event, yah? Now. Changing the subject. Dress code. Should we wear armour?"

"Knights should always wear armour," said Sir Percy. "We need to be prepared. In case of invasion."

"What – at a party?" Sir Prancelot squeaked.

"You never know," Sir Percy said darkly.

"*I* shan't be wearing armour," said Sir Tralahad. "It's a gig. I shall be wearing my minstrel gear."

"Jolly good," said Sir Prancelot. "Nice you're making the effort. I'm wondering whether to shave my moustache off. For a change. What about you, Sir Gary? What plans have you to mark this special occasion?"

"None," said Sir Gary. "I might not come."

Their voices faded. Aggie moved on.

She entered the meeting room, where Sir Angela was piling cups and saucers on the tray, which was swimming with cold tea. Mrs Spunge's biscuits hadn't been touched, apart from the one that lay on the floor.

"Sorry about the mess, Aggie," Sir Angela said. "They never think to clear up after themselves."

"That's all right, miss– Sir," said Aggie. "Leave it, I'll do it. When I've swept up."

"I'll help," said Sir Angela.

"That's all right, miss– Sir. It's my job."

"No, no," Sir Angela said. "I feel bad, leaving it all to you. You sweep and I'll do the cobwebs."

So Aggie swept, while Sir Angela drew her sword and dealt with the cobwebs.

*

So. In Castle Llamalot …

Mrs Spunge was in the throne room, having words with the Queen. The Queen was making all the right noises.

The King was strolling in the garden, chatting to Old Toby about shuffler beans (an Olde England version of runner beans). He was in a good mood, because he had managed to walk down the corridor without tripping over a single knight.

Shawn was hiding in the potting shed, hoping to avoid any more heavy lifting.

In the kitchen, Sir Bore de Gannet was rolling dough into a long, thin loaf while he waited for two large pots of water to come to the boil.

Sir Prancelot was looking in the mirror, trying to imagine his face without a moustache.

Sir Percy was working on his list of things to be done (but not by him).

Sir Tralahad was working on his table song. Verse three was giving him trouble. He could find nothing to rhyme with 'drop-leaf' apart from 'Stop Thief'. And why would a thief be stealing a table?

Sir Gary was staring out of the window, hoping for rain.

Bob was lolloping around the orchard, still on the hunt for Ethel.

Ethel had made it to the ramparts and was lying in a pool of sunlight, where she was being jeered at by ravens.

Chapter 5
Preparations

Time always goes slower than usual when you're looking forward to something exciting, like a fight, or a sleepover, or a trip to the seaside, or your first All Knight Party. It was just the same in olden times. The knights spent lots of time in their bed chambers standing before mirrors, thinking about how to look their best.

Everybody but Sir Gary had washed, in honour of the occasion. It was cold water, of course, but knights are used to that. Then they had moved on to the hair. (Not Sir Gary.) They had all tried out different styles, and ended up with the usual one, but done extra well. Then came the big decision. What to wear?

Sir Prancelot decided to go for a silvery, shiny, swashbuckling look with just a little armour. Light chain mail. Sword, but no helmet. He let his hair out and spent a lot of time brushing and tossing and fluffing. He spent even longer waxing his moustache. It had taken five years to grow, and he found he couldn't bear to part with it, even for a party. *Especially* for a party. Tonight, it would be at its most splendid.

Sir Percy was in full armour – the entire clanking caboodle. Everything was polished till it shone. You could see his face in his shield. He kept his helmet on, of course. Proper knights did. He was annoyed, because he hadn't been able to find Mrs Spunge to order the back-up jelly and buns and the all-important lemonade for toasting. Then he had found out that Sir Angela had already asked the kitchen wench. Without consulting Sir Percy first. When everyone knew he was in charge of running things. Annoying. Party or not, he would say something.

Sir Tralahad was in his stage gear – green doublet and hose, plus a folksy hat with a feather. He had put on a bit of weight since his last gig and the hose was a bit tight. And he still wasn't happy with verse three of the *Table-O!* song. Not that they'd notice. None of them liked music anyway. They might even talk all the way through it. His talent was wasted.

Sir Angela was drawing on her moustache and wondering whether or not to put a ribbon on her sword. Perhaps not. But she might add a plume to her helmet. She was rather looking forward to the party. It would make a change from just hanging about in the corridor, which is all they usually did.

Sir Angela was pleased with the nice job that she and Aggie had made of the new room. They had brought in candles and hung up a string of festive little flags and put out bunches of herbs to hide the old-vegetable smell. Well, they had to. Nobody else had. And you could bet the other knights wouldn't even say thank you. They thought that mood lighting and jolly party bunting appeared by magic, like swords in lakes.

Sir Gary wasn't bothering at all. He might go. He might not. He'd see how he felt, after a lie down.

While the knights were busy thinking, there was chaos down in the kitchen. Water was boiling over, snails and frogs were escaping, something was on fire in the oven and smoke and flour hung in the air like fog. In the midst of all this was a whirling dervish. Sir Bore de Gannet was skating around the greasy floor, singing French songs and doing twenty jobs

at once. He was in his element. This was the way the French cooked – with wild passion and complete abandon!

It was lucky there was no one to see the appalling mess he was making. Aggie was keeping out of the way and Mrs Spunge was in the best parlour, having a nice chat and a cup of tea with the Queen.

The King lay under the plum tree in the garden in a deck chair (Olde England fabric, no stripes). His mouth was open to catch flies, and he was enjoying the end of a blissful, knight-free day.

Over in the potting shed, Old Toby and Shawn were playing Snap, but they were ready to leap up and look busy the moment the King woke up.

Up on the ramparts, the sun dipped low. Ethel wondered about strolling down to try for early supper. See if the maniac with the buckets had left the kitchen. In a bit, maybe, no hurry. First, she'd have a bit of a snooze.

And Bob the castle dog? Well, he was doing something naughty. He had gone upstairs, where he wasn't allowed. For once, there was no one to shout at him. The corridors were empty. There was time to stop and sniff. Cock a leg on the empty metal man-shaped things standing on the stairs. Sharpen claws on the tapestries. Roll over on the rugs. Roam around the corridors, poking a nose into archways. Scratch at doors. Dog stuff.

That was how the day went. Tick … tock. Tick … tock.

Slow.

And then came the evening. Seven o'clock. Party Time!

Chapter 6
The All Knight Party!

Sir Prancelot was the first to arrive at the door of the new meeting room. His moustache was a joy to behold. It really should have had an entrance all of its own. It was combed and waxed to perfection. Never had it jutted out so fierce or so proud. Never had the tips been so pointy. What with that and the shiny silver get-up and the free-flowing hair and the sword and everything, Sir Prancelot felt he looked his best.

The door was closed. Sir Prancelot tried the handle.

Sir Bore de Gannet's voice came from within. "Go away," he said. "I tell you when to come in."

"What's happening?" Sir Tralahad asked, as he came up from behind, yanking up his hose. He had his lyre with him as well as a thick inky scroll with the words of *Table-O*. His minstrel hat was tilted to one side and the feather was tickling his nose, but he didn't have a free hand to scratch it. It wasn't the entrance he had hoped for.

"The feast's not quite ready, by the sound of it," Sir Prancelot said. "I say! Splendid hat, Sir Tralahad. What you would call a *knight cap*, yah? Ha, ha, hear what I said? I said, you would call it a *knight cap*."

"No," Sir Tralahad said. He had dropped the roll of parchment and was wondering whether to risk bending down for it. "I call it a hat."

"What's the problem here?" That was Sir Percy, clanking up to join them. "Did I hear you say not ready? We said seven o' the clock. What happened to time-keeping?" He rapped on the door with a metal fist. "I say! Open up! There are people waiting out here!"

"Patience!" Sir Bore de Gannet screamed from within. "You Engleesh! Always ze rush!"

"What's up?" Sir Angela said, from behind.

"He won't let us in yet," said Sir Prancelot. "Nice helmet plume, Angela. Sir AnGela, I mean. And I see you've drawn– grown your moustache again. Good gir– fellow!"

"Thanks," said Sir Angela.

"Sorry about earlier," Sir Prancelot said. "The chair and that."

"Forget it," said Sir Angela. "I've moved on."

"I want a word with you, Angela," said Sir Percy. "I mean, Sir AnGela. I hear you took it upon yourself to order the back-up jelly and buns and the lemonade for toasting. That was my job."

"Why, so it was!" Sir Angela said. "I clean forgot. Aggie and I were so busy cleaning and getting the room looking nice for tonight, for some reason I thought *everything* was down to us."

Sir Gary came squeaking down the corridor. He had made no effort at all. Hadn't even oiled his armour. He looked just the same as always. Fed up. Un-partyish.

"You're here, then," Sir Tralahad said in a cold voice.

"Yeah," said Sir Gary. "But I'm not staying long."

Sir Percy, still annoyed, raised his fist to bang on the door again. But there was no need. The door opened to reveal Shawn the odd job boy. His latest odd job had been to carry four heavy trays loaded with weird French food up three flights of stairs, and he wasn't at all happy.

"He says you can go in," Shawn growled, jerking his thumb.

"Our thanks, young feller-me-lad," Sir Prancelot cried. He reached out to do the hair-ruffling thing. Shawn ducked out of the way.

There was a chorus of "After you, Sir!" and "No, no, I insist, you first!" It was party time. Everyone was suddenly on their best, knightly behaviour.

Sir Gary cut to the chase and walked in.

The room looked good. Much, much better than they had left it this morning. Soft light from candles. Little flags hanging overhead. A nice, herby smell. An absence of spiders.

But Sir Angela and Aggie's hard work was overshadowed by the triumph that was Sir Bore de Gannet's French feast, all laid out on the new drop-leaf table.

Everybody's jaw dropped at the sight.

"Good grief!" Sir Prancelot gasped. "What is *that*?"

Sir Bore de Gannet stepped forward. He was still wearing his chef's hat and apron. He looked tired, but proud.

"Zat," Sir Bore de Gannet said, "zat, Sir, ees ze beautiful, flavoursome French food. Wiz my own twist."

"Well, yes, I'm sure it's *food*," Sir Percy snapped. "We can see bowls of sloppy stuff and stuff on plates and it's on a table, so it's clear it's food. But what *is* it?"

"Ze octopus soup," Sir Bore de Gannet said. "Ze frog-leg fricassée. Ze snail soufflé.

Ze crusty French loaf spread wiz a choice of ripe and steenky cheese or lizard liver pate. And for ze dessert – my speciality. Ze delicious lemon posset à la wasp!" With great drama, he pointed to a bowl full of yellow stuff with little stripy bits in.

A silence fell.

"Well," said Sir Angela, after a bit. "You've *arranged* it all very well."

Indeed, Sir Bore de Gannet had gone to great trouble when laying the table. The large, heavy bowls were set out on the fixed side. Smaller, lighter cold dishes were on the side with the dodgy drop-leaf, balanced with care so that the weight was even.

"Um – what's lemon posset-alla-wasp?" asked Sir Tralahad in a nervous voice.

"In Engleesh, you call eet sour custard," Sir Bore de Gannet explained. "Wiz wasps."

Another silence fell.

"What – real ones?" Sir Tralahad asked.

"Of course. Ees my own twist. You see, carefully, I remove ze stings," Sir Bore de Gannet said. He was getting all excited about his cooking skills. "And ze little legs. Zen I chop zem. Ze French way."

"I'm not eating any of that muck," said Sir Gary. "Chopped wasps? No chance."

"Zen don't 'ave dessert!" Sir Bore de Gannet snapped.

"I won't," said Sir Gary.

"I won't either, if you don't mind," Sir Tralahad said. "I'm singing tonight. Have to be careful of my throat."

"Your loss, Sirs! All ze more for ze rest of us. So!" Sir Bore de Gannet swept his hand over the groaning table. "'Oo will be first to try ze soup, before it get cold? Sir AnGela, can I tempt you? Frogs for you, Sir Prancelot? Come, form a line. Shawn, give out ze bowls. Pass me ze serving spoon."

A line didn't form. Forming a line and taking a bowl was commitment. Everyone looked at the ceiling or gave curt little head-shakes of refusal when Shawn tried to give them a bowl. Nobody wanted to try Sir Bore de Gannet's French food.

"Come on," Sir Bore de Gannet urged, waving his serving spoon around. "Zeez snails won't eat zemselves!"

"Why have you tucked the chairs in so that we can't sit down?" Sir Percy complained.

"No sitting," Sir Bore de Gannet explained. "Zis is a buffet."

"Huzzah!" Sir Prancelot cried, trying to lighten the mood. He felt that the party wasn't quite *there* yet. "A buffet! Awesome! Er – what's a buffet exactly?"

"You take a bowl," Sir Bore de Gannet said. "You 'elp yourself to food. You stand and eat eet."

"I've never heard of such a thing," Sir Percy said. "I hate to think what that does to the digestion. I prefer to put my bowl on a proper table and my bottom on a proper chair."

"Zere is no room at ze table, Sir!" Sir Bore de Gannet was clearly running out of patience. "As you see, it is covered wiz my beautiful food. Now. Are you eating or not?"

Just at that point, Aggie appeared with a tray full of jelly, back-up buns and lemonade. It was like the sun bursting forth on a cloudy day. This was more like it. There was a chorus of glad cries and a hungry surge towards the tray.

"What eez zis?" Sir Bore de Gannet demanded, clutching his brow. "Zis tray of 'orrible Engleesh wobbly stuff and spotty brown lumps and yellow bubble water?"

"Probably a mistake," Sir Angela said. "Someone forgot to cancel it, I expect."

"*Cancel* eet?" Sir Bore de Gannet shrieked. "Zis is an insult! What fool ordered it in ze first place?"

Sir Angela hesitated, but her eyes remained on Aggie's tray. She very much wanted a bun before they were all gone. Sir Percy kept toasting the King and Queen, so the lemonade was going down fast. But she felt a bit bad. After all, the French Feast had been her idea.

On the other hand, she hadn't expected tentacles. Or wasps.

Then again, Sir Bore de Gannet was hurt by their poor response to the food he'd prepared with such love.

"I have no idea who ordered it," Sir Angela lied. Knights weren't supposed to tell lies, but sometimes they did. "Tell you what, I'll

try a tiny piece of that long bread. And just a
weenzy splash of the soup."

Sir Bore de Gannet snatched her bowl and
poured in a large helping of octopus soup.
Tentacles hung over the side. Then he tore
off a hunk of bread and floated it on the top.
"Enjoy!" he cried. *Bon appetit!*

*

At that very moment, outside the party room,
Ethel the castle cat was making her way down
the corridor on her way to the kitchen.

Bob the castle dog had the same idea. He
was approaching from the other end of the
corridor.

They came face to face outside the door of
the new party room!

Ethel arched her back and hissed. Bob
crouched down and backed away, getting

ready to pounce. Just then, the door opened and Aggie came out, with an empty tray in her hands.

Ethel saw her chance. She shot like a furry cannon ball past Aggie's legs and into the room. Bob followed.

Well. It had to happen, didn't it?

CRRRRRRASH!

The noise of breaking plates was unbelievable. Crashing and shouting and spitting and snarling and barking! And a long string of words in French.

Aggie stared with her mouth open at the chaos. She looked down as a small river of octopus soup crept towards her shoes.

"Oops," she said. And she trudged off downstairs to collect the mop.

Chapter 7
The Stable Yard

"I suppose it had to happen sometime," Sir Angela said to Sir Prancelot. It was the morning after the party. They were sitting on a water butt in the stable yard. "The drop-leaf leg had to give way."

"Yah," Sir Prancelot agreed. "At least none of *us* can be held to blame."

They stared across the yard. Bob was tied to a hitching post, looking dejected. Ethel was sitting on a distant wall with her back turned, licking the last of the dried-up frog fricassée from her front paws. Both of them knew they were in deep trouble.

"It is a shame," Sir Tralahad said. "I didn't get the chance to sing *Table-O*."

"Good," said Sir Gary.

Sir Tralahad wondered whether to make a thing of it, but he decided he just couldn't be bothered.

"We'll have to do something about that drop-leaf, guys," Sir Prancelot said. "Can't have it collapsing like that. Could take someone's fingers off."

"Sir Percy's on the case," said Sir Angela. "He's up there now, getting Old Toby to fix it with glue."

"That won't work," said Sir Gary.

"Shouldn't someone go and cheer up Sir Bore de Gannet?" Sir Angela asked. "He hasn't said a word all morning."

They all looked over at Sir Bore de Gannet, who was sitting on his own in a corner, sulking.

"Let's ask him to come for a ride," Sir Prancelot cried. "Lovely morning for a merry charge through the forest. Hey! Sir Bore! Are you up for a ride, Sir?"

"*Non*," Sir Bore de Gannet snapped. "I wish to be alone."

"Ah, come on!" Sir Prancelot urged. "You can have first pick of the horses. Right, guys?"

"Right!" Sir Angela and Sir Tralahad agreed.

Sir Gary shrugged and said, "I'm not having Gnasher."

Sir Bore de Gannet looked over at the stalls where the horses waited.

Their names were Stop-a-lot, Lightning, Breakwind, Elton, Loud Winnie and Gnasher. Stop-a-lot stopped, a lot and with no warning. Lightning couldn't go slower if he tried. Breakwind broke wind. Elton was a girl. Winnie was noisy and Gnasher liked to bite.

Some horses were more popular than others. The knights often drew straws for who would ride who. The shortest straw always got Gnasher.

"Very well," Sir Bore de Gannet said. "I choose Elton." He was still upset, but he was tired of sitting by himself.

So they all went for a merry charge in the forest, and they all felt much better for it.

Except for Sir Gary, of course.

*

That night, the King and Queen sat up in bed together, having a chat.

"So," the King said. "How did the business with the room go?"

"Rather well," the Queen said. "They had an opening party last night, I believe. I think there was a bit of trouble with the table, and some sort of drama with the food. Sir Bore de Gannet cooked a French feast, I hear, but nobody ate it. Mrs Spunge is furious about the state of the kitchen. And there seem to be frogs hopping about everywhere. But on the whole, I think the room is a great success. At least it's keeping them out of the corridors."

"It is," the King agreed, "and long may it last. What a clever wife I've got."

He gave her a big smacker of a kiss and blew out the candle.

TABLE-O!

A song with 22 free-spirited verses

Gather round and hear my fable

All about a drop-leaf table,

Fal diddle dee and a ninny nonny no,

We're the knights of the drop-leaf table-o!

Some are round and some are square,

Ours is a drop-leaf! So there!

Fal diddle dee and a nonny no ninny,

T'was given to us by Good Queen Gwinny!

Stop, thief, stop, thief,

Bring back our drop-leaf,

Don't you steal our table-o!

Tis where we sit

And we're fond of it,

Shame it's a bit unstable, though.

With a hey nonny no and the wind and the rain,

My epic tale will now unfold,

Sing ho for the drop-leaf table-o!

The Queen, she had a good idea,

With a hey nonny no and the wind and the rain ...

Um ... ah ...

Oh, who cares anyway.

Our books are tested
for children and young people by
children and young people.

Thanks to everyone who consulted on
a manuscript for their time and effort in
helping us to make our books better
for our readers.